D0177531

For Benjamin Green

First published in Great Britain in 2009 by Andersen Press Ltd.,
20 Vauxhall Bridge Road, London SW1V 2SA.
Published in Australia by Random House Australia Pty.,
Level 3, 100 Pacific Highway, North Sydney, NSW 2060.
Copyright © Sarah Garson, 2009. The rights of Sarah Garson to be identified as
the author and illustrator of this work have been asserted by her in accordance
with the Copyright, Designs and Patents Act, 1988. All rights reserved.
Colour separated in Switzerland by Photolitho AG, Zürich.
Printed and bound in Singapore by Tien Wah Press.

10   9   8   7   6   5   4   3   2   1

British Library Cataloguing in Publication Data available. ISBN 978 1 84270 912 2

COVENTRY SCHOOLS LIBRARY SERVICE

| 08-Sep-2009 | JF |
| PETERS | |

One, Two, Cockatoo!

Sarah Garson

Andersen Press

1

One cockatoo on
his own in a tree.

2

Two cockatoos fly over . . .

3 ...that's three!

4 Four cockatoos
dancing a jive.

5 Another joins in and

hey-presto – that's five!

6 Six cockatoos huddled together.

7 Seven like splashing

around in wet weather.

8

Eight cockatoos

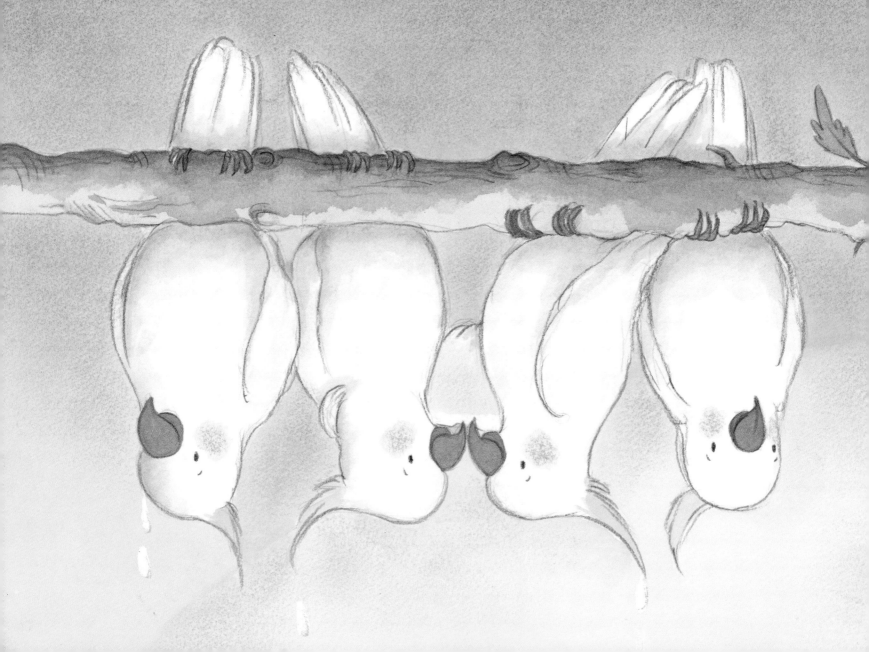

drying off in the sun.

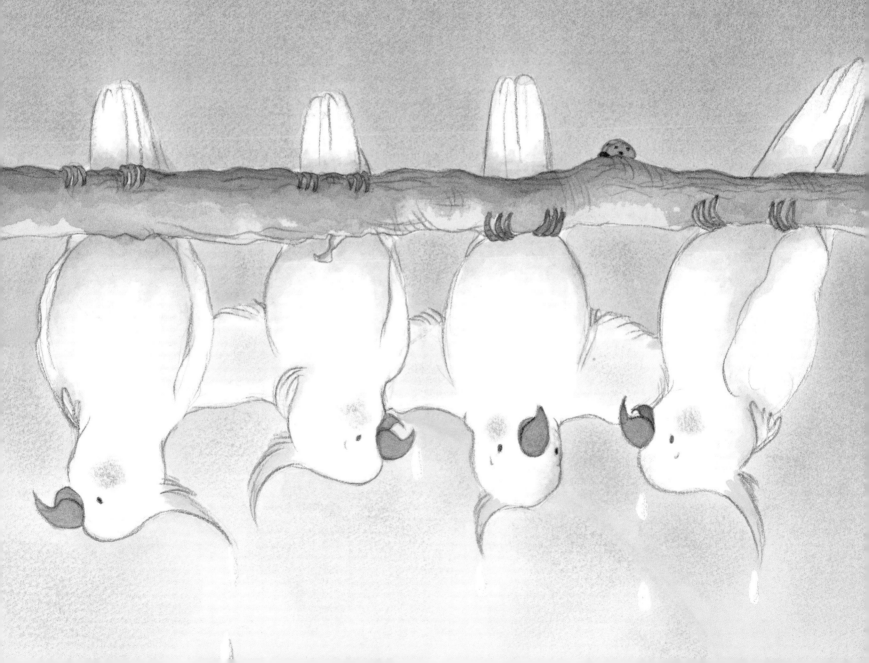

9 Nine cockatoos

playing peek-a-boo fun.

10 Ten cockatoos

and our story's complete . . .

...but hold on

...what's that?

Tweet, tweet, tweet, tweet!

3 8002 01826 2685